W9-AOL-733

The Berenstain Bears
and
THE TRUTH

No matter how you hope,
No matter how you try,
You can't make truth
Out of a lie.

A FIRST TIME BOOK®

The Berenstain Bears
and
THE TRUTH

Stan & Jan Berenstain

Random House 🏠 New York

Copyright © 1983 by Berenstains, Inc. All rights reserved under International and Pan-American Copyright Conventions. Published in the United States by Random House, Inc., New York, and simultaneously in Canada by Random House of Canada Limited, Toronto. *Library of Congress Cataloging in Publication Data:* Berenstain, Stan. The Berenstain bears and the truth. (First time books) SUMMARY: Brother and Sister Bear learn how important it is to tell the truth after they accidentally break Mama Bear's most favorite lamp. [1. Honesty—Fiction. 2. Bears—Fiction] I. Berenstain, Jan. II. Title. III. Series: Berenstain, Stan. First time books. PZ7.B4483Bel 1983 [E] 83-3304 ISBN: 0-394-85640-6 (trade); 0-394-95640-0 (lib. bdg.) Manufactured in the United States of America

24   25   26   27   28   29   30

It was a lazy sort of day in Bear Country. The air was so still that the leaves on the big tree house where the Bear family lived were hardly rustling.

Except in the beehive, where the bees were always busy, nothing much seemed to be happening.

It was the sort of day that sometimes leads to mischief.

Inside the tree house Brother and Sister
Bear were sitting around not doing anything
in particular.

Brother was holding his soccer ball—he'd become interested in soccer and had been outside practicing free kicks. Sister was relaxing in an easy chair, thinking about what to do next.

Neither Papa nor Mama Bear was around. Papa was in his shop working on some furniture, and Mama was out shopping.

"I know what," said Sister. "Let's go gather some wild blackberries."

Brother thought about that.

"No," he said, "wild black-berries have too many thorns, and besides, the seeds get stuck in your teeth."

"Well, then," said Sister, "let's go out and twist each other up on the swing and see who gets the dizziest."

Brother thought about that.

"No," he said. "That's silly, and besides, we did that yesterday."

Sister became irritated and impatient with her brother.

"My goodness!" she complained. "You don't want to do *anything*. All you want to do is sit there and hug that soccer ball. I think you must be in love with that soccer ball!"

"I am not!" protested Brother.
"But I'll tell you something—I bet
I can dribble this ball past you!"

Brother was a pretty good soccer player
and a *very* good dribbler. But so was Sister.

The only one who saw what happened next, besides the cubs, was a mockingbird who was perched on a twig outside an open window.

Brother faced Sister. The ball was on the floor between them. First Brother moved the ball with his right foot,

then with his left, trying to trick Sister out of position.

Then, quick as a flash, he gave the ball a sharp kick with his right.

It almost worked.

But Sister was fast too. She reached out with her knee and blocked the ball,

which bounced against a bookshelf,

against a chair,

against a footstool,

The mockingbird let out a screech and got out of there as fast as its wings could carry it. As it flew away it saw Mama Bear returning from the marketplace!

Now, the Bear family had some house rules just as any family has. One was "No honey eating in bed." Another was "No tracking mud on the clean floors." And another was *"No ball playing in the house"*!

What to do? Brother looked at Sister. Sister looked at Brother. They both looked at the broken lamp. And they both listened in horror as Mama came up the front steps and into the house.

All Brother had time to do before Mama came into the room was roll the ball behind Papa's chair.

"My lamp!" said Mama. "My best lamp! What happened?" she asked, looking into her cubs' eyes. "Tell me about it."

The cubs looked into Mama's eyes, then at each other, and then they began to tell one of the biggest whoppers that has ever been told in Bear Country.

"It was a bird!" began Brother. "Yes," added Sister, "a big purple bird with yellow feet!"

"And green wing tips,"
added Brother.

"And funny-looking red
feathers sticking out of its
head," said Sister, as a
finishing touch.

As most lies do, the purple bird
whopper got bigger and bigger and bigger.

"Yes," continued the cubs, "and it flew in that window, zoomed around the room, and knocked over the lamp!"

As Mama Bear was looking at the broken lamp with a sad expression on her face, Papa Bear came in from his shop.

The cubs began to tell him the story of the big bird that flew in the window and broke the lamp. It was harder to tell the second time. For one thing, they couldn't quite remember how they had told it the first time.

"You've got me confused," said Papa. "Was it a purple bird with green wing tips and yellow feet?

"Or a yellow bird with purple wing tips and green feet?

"*Or* . . . was it a white bird with black spots . . .

like that soccer ball behind my easy chair?"

But the thing that really made it hard the second time was how very sad Mama looked as she picked up the pieces of the broken lamp.

"Mama, we're really sorry about the lamp," said Brother.

"Oh, yes!" said Sister, picking up the last piece and putting it in the dust pan.

"Oh," said Mama, "I'm not worried about the lamp. We can always get another lamp, or we can glue this one back together. What I'm sad about is the thought that maybe, just maybe, my cubs, whom I've always trusted, aren't telling me the truth. And trust is not something you can put back together again."

Both cubs started to talk at once.
"It wasn't a bird!" said Sister. "It was a soccer ball."
"And it was all my fault!" shouted Brother.
"It was just as much my fault!" shouted Sister.

But they were both shouted down by the phone, which rang loudly.

It was Grizzly Gran
inviting the Bear family
for a Sunday visit.

"Hello, Gran!" said Mama. "Oh, everything
is just fine here in the tree house. How is
everything with you?"

"But, Mama!" protested Sister after Mama
hung up the phone. "You told Gran that everything is fine here, and that isn't really the truth."

"Oh, but it is," answered Mama. "We've got two fine cubs who have just learned a very important lesson about telling the truth. And what could be finer than that?

"Now, let's help Papa glue the lamp back together."

Nobody really expects cubs to be perfect, and from time to time Brother and Sister Bear did forget the rules.

Brother ate honey in bed a couple of times.

One time Sister tracked a little mud on the clean floor.

And once or twice Brother and Sister started to play ball in the house before they remembered not to.

But they never, ever again told a whopper . . .

because trust is one thing you can't put back
together once it's broken.